The Bullwinkl[e] Book

by Gale Wiersum

illustrations by Darrell Baker/Jason Studios

MERRIGOLD PRESS • NEW YORK

Bullwinkle and his friends are playing hide-and-seek. It's Rocky's turn to be "it," so he covers his eyes.

The others look for places to hide.

It's very hard for Bullwinkle to find a
place to hide. He is so big, and his antlers
are so long.

Mr. Peabody is a very smart dog. He knows good places to hide, like under a small, round table. The long, blue tablecloth hides him from view.

Bullwinkle tries to hide under an end table. But he is much too big, and his antlers won't even fit between the table legs.

Natasha is very good at hiding. Her favorite place to hide is in a closet.

Bullwinkle cannot hide in a closet. He tries, but his antlers get caught in the row of hangers.

It's easy for Boris to find a place to hide.
He is small enough to tuck himself neatly
behind a chair.

Bullwinkle cannot hide behind a chair.
He is too big, and his antlers stick way out.

Bullwinkle finally has an idea. "I'll make myself look like a coatrack!" he decides.

He takes everything off the real coatrack
in the living room.

He puts on Natasha's long, black coat.

Then he hangs a coat on each antler and one on his nose.

"Time's up!" shouts Rocky, uncovering
his eyes.

He finds Mr. Peabody.

Rocky finds Boris and Natasha. But he cannot find Bullwinkle.

Rocky searches everywhere, while Bullwinkle just stands very still in front of the
real coatrack.

Finally Rocky gives up. "All right, Bull-winkle. Come out, come out, wherever you are!"

"Here I am!" says Bullwinkle. He shakes
his head, and the coats fall to the floor.

He takes off Natasha's coat and grins at
Rocky's surprised face. Everyone else is
surprised, too!

"Bullwinkle, you're the best hide-and-seek player of all," says Rocky.

Bullwinkle smiles proudly and says,
"Thanks to my terrific antlers!"